A Dragon
in the Family

Don't miss the other adventures
of Darek and Zantor:

The Dragonling

Coming soon:

Dragon Quest

Dragons of Krad

Dragon Trouble

Dragons and Kings

The
DRAGONLING

A Dragon
in the Family

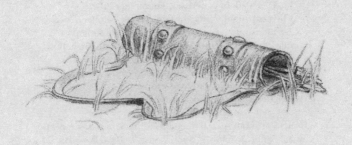

By Jackie French Koller

Illustrated by Judith Mitchell

ALADDIN
New York   London   Toronto   Sydney   New Delhi

ALADDIN
An imprint of Simon & Schuster Children's Publishing Division
1230 Avenue of the Americas, New York, New York 10020
This Aladdin paperback edition July 2018
Text copyright © 1993 by Jackie French Koller
Cover illustration copyright © 2018 by Tom Knight
Interior illustrations copyright © 1993 by Judith Mitchell
Also available in an Aladdin hardcover edition.
All rights reserved, including the right of reproduction in whole
or in part in any form.
ALADDIN and related logo are registered trademarks
of Simon & Schuster, Inc.
For information about special discounts for bulk purchases, please
contact Simon & Schuster Special Sales at 1-866-506-1949
or business@simonandschuster.com.
The Simon & Schuster Speakers Bureau can bring authors to your live
event. For more information or to book an event contact the
Simon & Schuster Speakers Bureau at 1-866-248-3049 or visit
our website at www.simonspeakers.com.
Designed by Laura Lyn DiSiena
The text of this book was set in ITC New Baskerville.
Manufactured in the United States of America 0618 OFF
2 4 6 8 10 9 7 5 3 1
Library of Congress Control Number 2017949640
ISBN 978-1-5344-0065-8 (hc)
ISBN 978-1-5344-0064-1 (pbk)
ISBN 978-1-5344-0066-5 (eBook)

For Bobby, who fights a Red Fanged
dragon with a sword made of courage
and a shield made of love

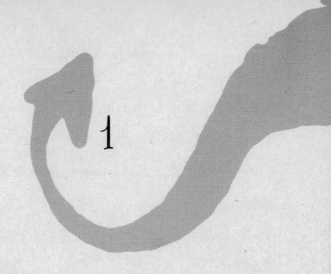

1

DAREK SAT ACROSS THE CAMPFIRE from his father, chewing but not tasting his food. It had been three days since their confrontation in the Valley of the Dragons, and still his father had hardly said a word to him. Would it be any different when they and the rest of their party reached home tomorrow? He glanced at his mother and his brother, Clep, and they each gave him a small reassuring smile. *Change takes time,* his mother kept telling him. *How much time?* Darek wondered. He longed for the day when his father would gaze upon him with love and pride again.

"Rrronk," came a sad cry from back in the shadows.

Darek's father looked up from his meal and frowned.

"I'll quiet him," said Darek, jumping up. He lit a torch and picked his way through the forest to the spot where the dragonling had been tied. He saw the green eyes shining in the night before he could make out the small form huddled beneath a zarnrod tree.

"Rrronk, rrronk," came the cry again.

"It's all right, Zantor," Darek called softly.

"Thrrummm," the creature sang happily when

he heard Darek's voice. He strained against the chain that held him fast.

Darek stuck his torch in the ground and quickly unlocked the collar. The soft blue scales underneath were torn, and the flesh was rubbed raw from the dragonling's efforts to free himself.

"I'm sorry, Zantor," Darek whispered, stroking the small bony head. "This is Father's idea. He still finds it hard to trust you, though I keep telling him you're no threat to the yukes or anything else."

Zantor nuzzled Darek, and Darek smiled. "Come, little friend," he whispered. "Let's find you some supper."

Darek lifted the torch and led the way down the path as the creature fluttered and danced around him, happy to be free. They came upon a patch of barliberry bushes, and Darek sat on a rock and watched while Zantor fed hungrily.

Darek still had to pinch himself sometimes, so strange did it seem to be friends with a dragon. He remembered how startled he had been that night, after the last dragonquest, when he had found the newborn in its dead mother's pouch. He hadn't known what to do. Watching the little dragon now, though, Darek knew he had made the right decision. Returning Zantor to the Valley of the Dragons had led Darek to an important discovery. The dragons, which he had been taught to hate and fear all his life, were not what they appeared to be. Fierce only when threatened, they wanted nothing more than to be left alone to live in peace.

When Darek had shared this news with the members of the search party who came after him, the women had welcomed it—no more of their sons would have to die in the ritual dragonquests. But the men were harder to convince. It had taken Bodak, whose son, Yoran, had died in the last dragonquest, to turn the tide.

Zantor shuffled over and dropped a cluster of barliberries in Darek's lap. Darek smiled and scratched the little dragon under his chin.

"I still can't believe Father is letting you come home with us," Darek whispered. "But then, how could he object when Bodak and Zilah offered to take you in, even knowing that your mother killed their son?"

The dragonling snuggled down against Darek's leg, and Darek pulled a berry from the clump in his lap and chewed it thoughtfully. Why was Father still angry? he wondered. The other villagers in their party seemed to see the value of befriending the dragons. There would be no more fighting, no more killing. The dragons and Zorians could help one another in many ways. Most exciting of all, the dragons could take the Zorians flying! Darek's eyes shone as he remembered his own flight in the pouch of a Great Blue.

Then, as quickly as it had come, his joy faded into worry again. Darek's father was Chief Marksman, an important man in the village, soon to join the Circle of Elders. What if the elders felt as he did? What if they accused Darek of treason? Treason was a serious crime.

Crime! Darek suddenly sat up straight, eyes wide, heart thumping. No wonder his father was so upset. Now Darek understood. Darek had been so preoccupied by the dragonling, he hadn't stopped to think that he might be committing a crime. In

Zoriak, if a child under the age of twelve committed a crime, it was the father who suffered the punishment! And Darek was only nine. A heavy weight settled in his chest. Much as he loved the little dragon, he loved his father more. The last thing he wanted was to get him in trouble.

Darek heard a soft *"flubba bub bub bub, flubba bub bub bub."* He looked down to see the dragon curled up, gently snoring, his chin resting on Darek's foot. Darek sighed. His heart felt like the rope in a tug-of-war, pulled first this way, then that, until it was ready to snap.

"Why did my brother have to kill your mother?" he whispered to the sleeping dragon. "Why did your mother have to kill Yoran?"

"Flubba bub bub bub" was the dragon's only response, but Darek stared up at the night sky and

found his answer in the cold and silent stars. The killings had happened because the killings had always happened, and unless Darek could make a change, the killings would go on and on and on. . . .

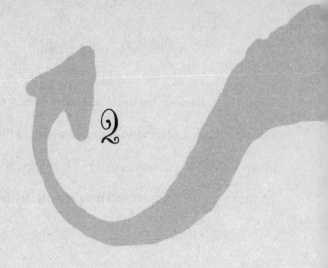

2

DAREK COULD HEAR THE VILLAGE bell clanging while he and the others were still some distance from town. The lookout had obviously caught sight of them. By the time they reached the bottom of the mountain pass, the village square was filled with people.

"Hooray!" the villagers shouted when they caught sight of Darek. "The boy has been found. The boy is well!" Then, on the heels of their cheers came another sound. A gasp of surprise swept through the crowd. "A dragonling!" Darek heard. "There's a dragon with him!"

Darek pulled in Zantor's chain, keeping him close. The crowd and the noise were making the creature skittish, and Darek wanted no problems. His father was already upset enough, staring straight ahead, stony faced as he strode along beside Darek. What was going through his father's mind? Darek wondered. What fate awaited them all?

"Darek! Darek!"

Darek whirled at the sound of the familiar voice. "Pola? Pola, where are you?" Darek searched for his best friend in the sea of faces around him.

"Here. Over here." A hand waved frantically, then Pola burst through the crowd and rushed up and threw his arms around Darek. "You're safe!" he cried.

"Yes, yes, I'm fine. . . ."

"What happened? They say you went to the Valley of the Dragons. They say—"

Suddenly Pola stopped talking and pulled back. He stared oddly at Darek. "By the twin moons of Zoriak," he whispered, "what happened to you?" He pointed at Darek's belly.

Darek looked down. In his excitement over seeing his friend, he hadn't noticed that Zantor had somehow wiggled in between them and shoved his head up under Darek's tunic, making Darek look like a four-legged, blue-tailed beast that was about to deliver a baby.

Darek laughed in spite of his fear. "Will you

get out of there?" he whispered, pushing Zantor's head down and out.

"*Rrronk!*" cried the little beast. He ducked between Darek's legs and shoved his head up under the back side of the tunic.

Darek grinned, red faced, at Pola. "It's—it's a dragon," he stammered. "He—uh—thinks I'm his mother."

"A what?!" Pola took another step back.

"It's okay," Darek hurried to say. "He's harmless. See?" He gently pushed the dragon out from under his tunic again and coaxed him around front. "That's a good boy," he murmured, rubbing the knobby head affectionately.

"DAREK!"

Darek jumped, and the dragonling dived between his legs and up under his tunic again.

Darek turned in the direction of his father's voice and saw that the crowd had parted to let Darek's father, Yanek, pass. His father and the Chief Elder waited up ahead in the village square. "Bring the beast forward," his father yelled.

Darek gulped. "I gotta go," he whispered nervously to Pola. "I'll explain later." He hurried forward, dragging the baby dragon along behind.

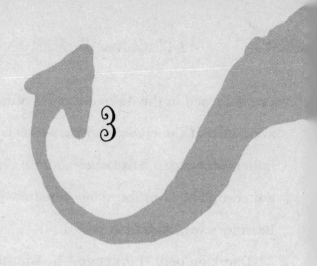

3

DAREK STARED UP INTO THE STERN eyes of the Chief Elder and blurted out the whole story—how he had found the newborn dragon and taken him back to the Valley of the Dragons, how a Great Blue dragon had befriended them, and finally, how he had placed himself between the dragons and the Zorian rescue party in order to avert a battle.

"The dragons let us go unharmed," Darek

ended breathlessly. "Don't you see? They didn't want to fight. They don't like to fight. They only fight to protect their young."

The Chief Elder's hard expression never wavered. If he found any of this news surprising, he gave no sign. All around them the villagers crowded close, murmuring in hushed tones and waiting for the Chief's reaction. Overhead the violet rays of the Zorian sun beat down. Beads of sweat began to trickle down Darek's neck and back.

Suddenly Darek felt something tickle between his shoulder blades. He twitched and tried to ignore it, but it came again. Zantor, still hiding under the back of Darek's tunic, was licking the droplets of salty sweat with his scratchy tongue. Darek twitched again and tried to hold back a giggle, but it was no use. The more he twitched, the more the little tongue flicked. At last Darek could stand it no more. He burst out laughing and crumpled up in a heap of hysterics, rolling and kicking on the ground, trying to get away from the tickly tongue. The more Darek laughed, though, the more Zantor seemed to think it was all a great game, and no sooner would Darek roll free than the little beast would pounce again, seeking out another bare patch of skin to tease. Round and round in the dust they rolled, laughing and thrumming, wiggling and tickling until at last they both lay still, too exhausted to move another muscle.

Darek lay on his stomach in the dirt, still giggling in little bursts and trying to catch his breath when he noticed the sea of boots and clogs around him.

"Uh-oh," he mumbled, remembering where he

was and why. He slowly rolled over and looked up.

The Chief Elder's eyes were hard as granite, and Darek's father's face was crimson, but, Darek noted with some relief, many of the other villagers were smiling.

"Rise!" the Chief's voice boomed.

Darek scrambled to his feet, and the dragon darted behind him and dived under his shirt again. The Chief Elder's face wrinkled in disgust. He turned to a pair of guards who stood nearby.

"Take the beast to the guardhouse," he said.

"The guardhouse!" Darek cried, his arms shielding the dragon. "No, you can't!"

The Chief Elder nodded to the guards, and they began to circle Darek.

"No. Please," Darek argued, circling too, trying to keep his body between the dragonling and the

guards. "You don't understand. He'll be terrified."

One of the guards lunged and grabbed Zantor by the tail.

"Rrronk! Rrronk!" the dragonling yowled, digging his claws into Darek's back.

"Ouch! Stop! Please! He's clawing me! Aaagh!"

The guard went on pulling, the dragon went on clawing, and Darek went on screaming until at last Darek heard his mother yell, "Yanek, for the sake of Lord Eternal, do something!"

Darek's father finally stepped forward and gave the guard a shove that sent him sprawling backward into the dust. Gasps of surprise rippled through the crowd, but Darek hardly noticed, intent on freeing himself from Zantor's frantic clutches. At last he coaxed the dragonling out from under his tunic.

"It's okay, Zantor. It's okay," he whispered. "I won't let them take you away." Zantor shivered and nuzzled his head against Darek's chest.

Darek's father went over and extended a hand to help the fallen guard to his feet, then he turned, his face crimson again, and bowed to the Chief Elder.

"A thousand pardons, Sire . . . ," he began.

"Silence!" The Chief Elder gestured to the guards. "Throw him in the guardhouse too!" he bellowed.

The guards grabbed hold of Darek's father, but before they could take him away, Darek's mother rushed up and linked arms with her husband. Bodak and his wife, Zilah, quickly joined them, then another woman and another man did as well. Soon the whole rescue party stood arm in arm. Darek's father seemed startled, and deeply touched.

"Sire," he said, his voice stronger now, "my son speaks the truth. Those of us who followed him to the Valley of the Dragons have seen it for ourselves. The time has come to talk."

4

AN IMMEDIATE MEETING OF THE Circle of Elders was called. Darek's father and Bodak were commanded to attend.

"What do you think will happen?" Darek and his brother, Clep, asked their mother as they made their way home, trailed very closely by Zantor.

"I don't know," she said simply. "We'll just have to wait and see."

"But can't we do something in the meantime?" Darek begged.

"Yes," said his mother. "We can do the chores. Lord Eternal knows they've been left waiting long enough."

Zantor stepped on Darek's heel. Darek staggered a few feet, then regained his balance. He turned and glared down at the dragonling, who bumped smack into him again in his haste to catch up. All this togetherness was beginning to get on Darek's nerves. "Is it necessary to walk on my feet?" he snapped.

The little dragon stared up at him a moment in surprise, then—*thwip!*—out darted the forked tongue, planting a tickly little dragon kiss right on Darek's lips.

Darek rolled his eyes skyward, and Clep and

their mother burst out laughing. Darek couldn't help laughing too, which made Zantor do a happy little shuffling jig.

"That's the way," said Darek, nodding to the dragon. "Practice being cute. You're going to need all your tricks when Father comes back and finds we've brought you home with us."

"Well," said Darek's mother, "I don't see what choice we had, other than sending you off to live with Bodak and Zilah too."

Darek's smile faded and he sighed. "I fear Father will think that the better choice," he said.

Darek's mother slid an arm around his shoulders as they walked. "Don't you believe that," she said. "Not for a moment. Your father may be worried and confused, but he still loves you very much."

"Enough to put up with a dragon in the family?" asked Darek.

Darek's mother reached over and patted the little horn nubs on Zantor's head. "Yes," she said, "I think so . . . in time."

"In time?" Darek frowned. "But what are we to do *now*? Father will be back in a little while."

They had reached home, and Darek's mother pushed open the garden gate and looked over at the messy, neglected barnyard. "I think chores would be a *very* good idea," she said.

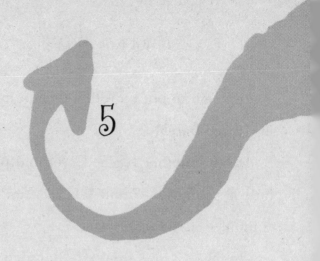

5

FORTUNATELY, MOST OF THE YUKES

had new calves, so they had not suffered for lack of

milking. The zok eggs had piled up some, though,

and were beginning to smell. The zoks squawked

and scolded as Darek and Clep reached into their

nests and gathered up the eggs.

"*Rrronk, rrronk,*" cried Zantor when the boys

carried two brimming basketfuls of foul-smelling

eggs out of the zok house. They carried them

down near the river, then went to get shovels. But by the time they had returned, Zantor had already dug a deep hole and pushed the eggs in. As the boys watched, he neatly covered the hole over again.

"Wow," said Clep. "He's pretty handy to have around."

"I told you," said Darek. "Imagine the things a big one could do. It could plow up a field in no time!"

"Yeah," said Clep thoughtfully. "Or dig irrigation ditches."

"Or help in the zitanium mines," added Darek.

"Or dig a swimming hole," said Clep, eyes shining. Darek and Clep had always dreamed of having their own swimming hole.

"Sure," said Darek as they picked up their

shovels and headed back to the paddock. "All we'd have to do is feed them."

"Feed them!" Clep wrinkled up his brow. "Did you happen to notice how big they get?"

"Of course I did. But with all their help we could easily raise enough food."

Clep still looked skeptical.

"Wanna see something else?" said Darek. He picked up a couple sticks and placed them on the ground. Immediately Zantor started shuffling around and nudging more sticks into the pile. When the pile was just the right size for a campfire—*whoosh!*—a stream of flame shot out of the little dragon's mouth and set it all ablaze.

"Wow," Clep repeated.

"That's nothing," said Darek, and he launched into the story of how he had flown in the pouch of a Great Blue, high above the Valley of the Dragons. Darek had already told Clep the story, several times in fact, on the journey back from the valley, but Darek could see that Clep was only just now beginning to believe it. Darek smiled, thinking how hard it would be for him to believe if it hadn't actually happened to him.

"It's like nothing you've done in your life before, Clep," he said wistfully. "They are the most magnificent creatures!"

Clep stared at Darek a moment, then looked away.

"What's wrong?" asked Darek.

"Nothing," said Clep.

"Yes there is. I can see it. Tell me, Clep. Please."

Clep kicked another stick into the fire and shoved his hands into his breeches. "It's just that . . . well, a couple days ago I was a hero, a Marksman. Now I feel like a murderer. You've changed everything, Darek. I don't know what I am anymore."

SPLAT!

A zok egg came flying over the paddock wall and hit Darek square in the middle of the forehead.

SPLAT! SPLAT! A shower of rotten, rank-smelling zok eggs followed, pelting Darek, Clep, and Zantor.

"Traitors!" they heard. "Dragon lovers!"

Darek and Clep tried to protect themselves, but the eggs were coming too fast. The sticky yolks dripped in their eyes and blinded them. The smell made them gag. Then there was another sound, something between a *rrronk* and *grrrawk* followed by frightened yells and running footsteps, and the egg shower stopped.

Darek wiped the egg from his eyes and stared. Zantor was perched atop the paddock wall, wings spread, claws unsheathed, flames shooting from his mouth in a full dragon battle stance.

Darek and Clep raced to the wall in time to see a gang of young Zorian boys retreating over the nearest hill.

"Wow," said Clep, staring up at Zantor in awe. "I didn't think he had it in him. Did you ever see him act like that?"

Darek didn't answer. He was still staring at the hill.

"Darek," said Clep, "what's wrong?"

"I saw one of them," said Darek quietly. "It was Pola."

6

"TRY TO UNDERSTAND," SAID CLEP. "I probably would have done the same thing a week ago. The truth is, so would you."

Darek scrubbed the last of the rotten egg from his face, then bent down and ducked his head under the water again. Clep was right, he knew. Zorian boys spent years training for their dragon-quests. If someone had tried to tell him just last week that everything had changed, that he would never get to go on his, he would have been furious. He waded in toward the riverbank, shaking the water from his hair. Clep tossed him a drying cloth.

"Maybe you're right," Darek admitted, "but I never would have done anything like this to Pola. Never. He didn't even let me explain."

"Maybe it wasn't him," said Clep. "Maybe it was just somebody who looks like him from the back."

"Yeah," said Darek. "Maybe you're right." It made him feel better to believe that, even if it wasn't the truth.

Zantor still frolicked in the river, and the two brothers stood on the bank and watched him for a moment, deep in thought.

"It's all going wrong," said Darek quietly. "I thought everyone would be happy. I thought it would be so easy."

"I knew it wouldn't be easy," said Clep, "but it's the right thing to do."

Darek looked up at his big brother in surprise. "Do you really believe that?" he asked.

Clep nodded and clapped Darek on the shoulder. "Yes, I do." He smiled at his little brother's astonishment. "I even heard Bodak tell Father that he thinks you have the makings of a great leader."

"Bodak said that?"

Clep nodded, and Darek thought quietly for a moment. "What answer did Father make?" he asked.

Clep avoided his eyes. "There's the dinner bell!" he said quickly, seeming glad of a reason to change the subject. "Hurry and get dressed now."

Darek and Clep closed Zantor up in the barn with a pile of barliberries and a promise to return quickly, and to their surprise, he did not protest. He seemed to sense that this was home now. When they got to the kitchen, their father was already there. His face was grim and Darek's heart squeezed with fear. He longed to ask what had happened at the Circle, but his voice would not come out.

Clep started to ask, but a glance from their mother silenced him.

"Let your father have dinner," she said, "then we'll talk."

They ate in silence, Darek and Clep stealing worried glances at each other and at their father's somber face. At last Yanek pushed his plate away and lit his pipe. He sucked in deeply, then blew a long column of smoke from his lips.

"Is the beast with Zilah?" he asked.

Darek glanced nervously at Clep and their mother. "N-no," he stammered. "He wouldn't go with her. He's in the barn."

Darek's father nodded tiredly as if he'd expected as much, then went on smoking his pipe in silence. At last Darek couldn't stand the suspense any longer.

"What did the Circle decide?" he blurted out. "What was the vote?"

Darek's father took the pipe from his lips. "The Circle voted to put the beast to death," he said.

A cry of protest sprang instantly to Darek's lips, but his father held up a finger for silence. "I'm not through," he chided.

Darek nodded obediently, and his father went on.

"Bodak and I convinced the Circle that the beast deserves a trial," he said.

Darek's eyes opened wide in wonder. "You did?"

"Yes."

"But . . . why would you? I mean, I thought you didn't . . ."

Darek's father took another long puff on his pipe. "I'm a fair man," he said, then smiled at his wife and added, "if not always the most flexible one."

Darek's mother reached over and squeezed her husband's hand. "True on both counts," she said with a wink at Darek.

The great weight of the past few days began to lift from Darek's heart, but Clep still looked worried.

"What manner of trial do the elders have in mind?" he asked.

"Simply this," Yanek answered. "The beast can live among us until the first sign of trouble."

"And if there *is* trouble?" Clep inquired.

Darek's father glanced at the faces of his wife and sons, then lowered his eyes. "*Then* he will be put to death," he said quietly, "and so will Bodak and I."

7

DAREK SAT ON A BALE OF ZORGRASS
watching Zantor try to perch on a yuke stall like a
zok. It was obvious that the dragonling was doing
his best to make Darek laugh, but Darek's heart
was too heavy. How could this be happening? he
wondered. How could an act of love and caring get
twisted into such a nightmare?

"It isn't fair," he cried out. "It just isn't fair!"

"What isn't fair?"

Darek turned and saw his father standing in the doorway. Darek turned away again, fighting with all his might to hold back the tears. "Nothing," he said softly.

There were footsteps, and then Darek felt a hand on his shoulder.

"Mind if I sit down?"

Darek looked up, and then the tears stung his eyes and slid down his cheeks. "Oh, Father," he whispered. "I'm so sorry."

Darek's father sat down next to him, leaned his elbows on his knees, and clasped his hands together tightly.

"No, son," he said. "I am the one who is sorry."

"You?" Darek started to protest, but Yanek held up a finger to silence him.

"Hear me," he commanded.

Darek wiped his eyes and nodded.

"I have treated you badly," Yanek went on. "In truth, the anger I have shown to you these past few days was really anger and contempt for myself."

Darek stared at his father in astonishment. "But why?" he asked.

Yanek rubbed his forehead tiredly. "Because in my heart I have known for a long time the truth about the dragons, and I have denied it."

Darek's mouth fell open in disbelief, and Yanek shook his head as if irritated with himself. "In the old days," he went on, "when the Red Fanged and Purple Spiked dragons roamed the valley, our fathers were great warriors. Their skills protected their families. Their deeds of valor gave them places of honor in our society. They fought until the Reds and Purples were gone."

Yanek fell silent, and Darek stared at him in confusion. "Then what happened?" he asked.

Darek's father sighed. "What is a warrior without a war?" he asked. "Somehow all dragons became the enemy. Green Horned, Yellow Crested, Great Blue . . . What matter that their kind never bothered our villages? What matter that they had not even a taste for flesh? When a man wants to be a hero, he needs a foe to vanquish."

Darek looked over at Zantor, who had finally accomplished the task he had set for himself and sat staring at them proudly like an oversize blue zok. The sight was so comical that Darek might have laughed if he hadn't felt so heartsick.

"Then it's all been a lie," he said. "All the training, all the battles, all the deaths . . ."

Yanek nodded slowly. "Yes," he said, "and that's why what you have done is so dangerous."

"Dangerous?" Darek repeated.

"Yes," said his father. "I'm afraid our whole society is built around this lie, and those who have gained the most from it will fight hardest to keep the truth a secret."

"You mean . . . the Circle of Elders," said Darek.

"Yes," said Yanek.

"But how?" asked Darek. "How can they fight this?"

"The same way they always have, my son. By making the lie appear to be true, so true that they can believe it themselves."

"How can they do that?"

There was a sudden commotion out in the

yard, followed by the sound of many voices raised in anger.

Darek's father stiffened. "I fear we are about to see how," he whispered.

"Yanek!" a voice boomed. "Yanek of Zoriak, come forth!"

8

DAREK'S FATHER WAS GRABBED BY A
guard as soon as he and Darek emerged from the
barn. His arms were shackled behind his back,
and he was pushed over to where Bodak stood,
shackled as well. A great crowd of villagers had
assembled in the paddock, and the Circle of
Elders stood at its center.

"What's wrong?" Darek cried. "What are you
going to do with my father?"

"Silence!" the Chief Elder boomed. "Where are you hiding the beast?"

"The beast?" said Darek, so frightened that for a moment he couldn't think what the Chief Elder meant.

"Don't play the fool!" the Chief bellowed. "We know . . ."

He never had to finish his sentence, for at that moment a zok strutted out of the barn, and right behind it strutted Zantor, doing the silliest zok imitation Darek had ever seen.

No one was amused.

"He's there!" came a panicky cry. "Watch out! Seize him!"

Shrieks of fear rang out on all sides, and before Darek knew what was happening, Zantor was snagged in a chain-mail net. A zitanium cage was rolled up, and the little creature was tossed inside.

"Rrronk! Rrronk!" he cried out.

Now that the dragonling was safely locked up, a group of children began to tease and taunt him, poking him with sticks and tossing stones into the cage. Zantor's *rrronks!* became shrill *grrrawks!* He unsheathed his claws and began charging at the bars, arrows of flame shooting from his mouth.

"Do you see?" screamed a hysterical mother to the elders. "Is it not as I said?"

The Chief Elder nodded slowly. His face was stern, but it was obvious that he was well pleased with the events that were taking place before him.

At that moment Darek's mother burst out of the house, followed by Clep.

"What's going on?" she cried, staring wildly at the scene before her. "What's happened?"

"I fear, Madam," said the Chief Elder, "that the beast has attacked a group of boys unprovoked. Friends of your son, I believe."

Darek's eyes widened. "That's a lie!" he shouted.

"A lie?" The Chief Elder turned toward Darek. He smiled slowly and snapped his fingers. "Bring the boys here," he called over his shoulder. Two mothers came forward with two boys Darek knew, but not well.

"See for yourself," said the Chief.

The boys turned, and Darek saw that their clothes were scorched and their hair singed. The chief gave Darek a smug look.

"They're not friends!" Darek cried. "They

tried to hurt me and Clep. Zantor was just defending us."

The Chief turned a deaf ear to Darek's pleas. "Take the prisoners to the council house!" he shouted. "Let the trials begin!"

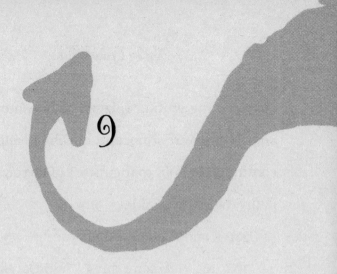

9

DAREK STARED HELPLESSLY AS
Zantor continued to thrash and roar in his cage
outside the council house. Now and then the
dragonling made a new sound, an earsplitting
eeeiiieee! If found guilty, Zantor would be the lucky
one, though. He would simply be target practice
for the archers. Darek's father and Bodak would
be burned at the stake.

Darek's mother and Zilah tried desperately to

convince the waiting villagers that Zantor, Yanek, and Bodak were innocent, but the group of boys continued to hold to their story of terror, and sympathy was on their side.

Darek and Clep paced nervously.

"I've got to *do* something," said Darek. "I can't just wait here like this."

"Haven't you done enough already?" Clep snapped.

Darek stopped pacing and stared at his brother. "Are you blaming me, Clep?" he asked quietly.

"Yes . . . No." Clep put his hands over his face. "I don't know what to think anymore. I just want it to be a bad dream. I want to wake up and find out that it's just an ordinary day and we're all going fishing like we used to, me and Yoran, and you and Pola—"

"Pola!" Darek grabbed Clep by the shoulders and stared into his eyes. "Pola was with them, remember? Pola knows the truth!"

Clep stared back for a moment, then shook his head. "You're not sure of that," he said, "and even if he was with them, what makes you think he'll tell the truth?"

Darek stared over Clep's shoulder at Zantor. "He'll tell," he whispered. "I'll *make* him tell."

Darek found Pola out behind his house, shooting arrows aimlessly into the air.

"Pola!" he shouted. "Pola, we've got to talk!"

Pola glanced over his shoulder at Darek, frowned, and looked away again. He loosed another arrow, watching its lazy flight.

"Pola, listen to me!" Darek ran up behind

his friend, grabbed his arm, and whirled him around.

"Hey," Pola growled, pulling his arm free. "Leave me alone."

"No!" Darek shouted. "You've got to help me."

"Help you do what?" asked Pola sullenly.

Darek stared at him. "Haven't you heard?" he asked. "Don't you know?"

"Know what?" asked Pola.

"They're trying my father," shouted Darek, "and my friend Zantor." Darek narrowed his eyes. "You know," he added dryly, "the fierce dragon who attacks young boys unprovoked."

Pola's eyes widened, then he looked away.

"I—I don't know what you're talking about," he said.

"No?" Darek grabbed the hat from Pola's head

and clutched a handful of singed hair. "Then how did you get this?"

Pola said nothing.

"Answer me, Pola!"

"I—I never meant to hurt your father," mumbled Pola. "I just wanted to get the dragon."

Darek let go of Pola's hair and handed him his hat. "Why?" he asked angrily. "What did the dragon do to you?"

Pola whirled away and slammed his bow to the ground. "It doesn't belong here!" he shouted. "It changes everything, don't you see? All the training, the matches, the tournaments, all the games of skill we've played all our lives! None of them matter anymore."

Darek stared at the bow lying between them on the ground. He wanted to hate Pola, but he couldn't. He understood Pola's feelings too well. In his heart he knew he would have felt the same way once.

A great clamor of voices rose up, carried on the wind from the village square. Time was running out. Darek had to win Pola to his side now. He grabbed up the bow and found an arrow that lay nearby. He fitted the arrow to the string and surveyed the meadow. Far away on the opposite side stood a young purple sapling. Reaching it would be quite a stretch, but Darek had to try. He tilted the bow up and let fly. He watched, holding his breath as the arrow arched out high over the meadow, then dropped slowly and . . . struck! Praise Lord Eternal. His aim was true.

Darek lowered the bow and looked at Pola. His friend was envious of the shot, he could tell.

"Here," he said, holding out the bow. "Match that."

"What?"

"Match it," Darek repeated.

"Why?" asked Pola, narrowing his eyes.

"Because you want to," said Darek. "Admit it. Whether you ever fight a dragon or not, you *want* to shoot, because you want to prove you're as good as me. That's where the fun lies, Pola. In the competition, not the killing. Match it. I dare you."

Pola stared at Darek a long time, then silently took the bow and pulled an arrow from his quiver. Slowly he turned, fitted the arrow to the string, and took aim. Darek held his breath again as the arrow arched out over the meadow, going higher, higher, then lower, lower, and . . .

"Yah!" shrieked Pola, tossing his hat into the air.

The boys clutched each other in a brotherly hug as their arrows quivered side by side far across the meadow.

10

DAREK WAS PREPARED FOR A GUILTY

verdict, but he was not prepared for the sight that greeted him when he and Pola reached the square. The executions had begun! Yanek and Bodak were lashed to their stakes, and archers were lining up in front of Zantor's cage.

"Stop!" Darek shrieked as he and Pola tried to push their way through the crowd. "Stop! It's all a mistake!"

No one listened. No one cared. Everyone was too busy watching the show, shouting and jeering.

"Stop!" the two boys cried together. "Somebody listen, please!" Darek pushed and shoved at the crowd, but he was making no headway. He pushed at a big man who pushed him back and sent him sprawling in the dust. Darek scrambled to his feet again, grabbed a rock, and motioned for Pola to follow. He got as close as he could to the platform where the village bell sat, then let the rock fly.

CLANG . . . ANG . . . ANG!

All heads turned as Darek hoisted himself up onto the platform and pulled Pola up too.

"Stop!" Darek yelled. "This is all a mistake! We've got to stop the executions now!"

The Chief Elder gave a signal, and the guards

touched flaming torches to the piles of brush that circled Yanek and Bodak.

"NO!" Darek cried. "These men are innocent!"

"It's true," Pola shouted. "I was among the boys." He turned so people could see his singed hair, then turned back and hung his head in shame. "We attacked Darek and Clep," he went on. "We provoked the beast!"

Mouths dropped open and a hush fell over the crowd. Then, "He's lying!" someone shouted.

"Aye! Aye!"

"No!" Pola cried. "It's the truth." He scanned the crowd before him. "Malek!" he said suddenly. "Dorwin!" He pointed to the two boys who had brought the charges. "Tell them! This has gone too far."

All eyes turned toward the two boys. They

stared at each other uncomfortably for a moment, then slowly nodded and hung their heads. The crowd gasped.

"Don't you see?" shouted Darek. "The only lie is that the dragons are our enemies! Do they attack our villages? Do they raid our herds? No! They fight only when we attack them, only when they are provoked!"

Darek could see that he had the attention of the crowd now. He pointed to where his mother and Zilah stood. "Zilah's son is dead," he said, "and so is my mother's brother. How many others of you have lost sons, brothers, husbands, or fathers?"

People murmured together, then a hand went up, followed by another, and another. Darek watched until almost everyone had a hand in the air. "Look!" he shouted. "Turn your heads and *look*, and then decide. . . . How many more must die for the sake of a lie?"

Heads swiveled, then hands were slowly lowered and shoulders sagged in sorrow. The silence was heavy, broken only by Zantor's shrill screams. Then came another tortured cry.

"Aa-a-gh!"

"Yanek! Bodak!" someone yelled. "Water! Hurry!"

The crowd came to life, and people flew in all directions, but time was running out. Bodak and Yanek writhed in agony as flames licked at their legs.

"Eeeiiieee!" shrieked Zantor. *"Eeeiiieee!"*

The pitch of Zantor's shrieks became so high that people in the crowd began to clasp their ears and cry out in pain. Then, as Darek watched in astonishment, Zantor's cage shattered like a crystal shell, and the little dragon rose up into the air. He fluttered over and dropped down into the ring of flame that surrounded Darek's father. A moment later the dragonling rose up again, tiny wings pumping furiously. Darek's father's great limp body was clutched tightly in his claws.

Darek's father and Bodak sat sipping hot glub from steaming mugs, their bandaged feet propped up on chairs. Zantor was curled up in exhausted sleep between them, and Yanek reached down and stroked his small head affectionately.

The little dragon stirred. *"Thrrummm,"* he mumbled tiredly.

Bodak smiled. "You know, Yanek," he said, "I still can't quite believe I'm sitting here."

Yanek nodded and looked over at Darek. Love

and pride glowed in his eyes. "Aye," he said, shaking his head in wonder, "neither can I, but I guess when you have a son who has the makings of a great leader, anything is possible."

Darek smiled back, warmed by his father's words, but a little bit frightened, too. Leadership, he had discovered, could be a pretty scary business. Maybe he *would* be a leader someday, but for now he just wanted to be a boy again, a boy with a dragon in the family.

**Turn the page for a peek
at the next book in the series:**

Dragon Quest

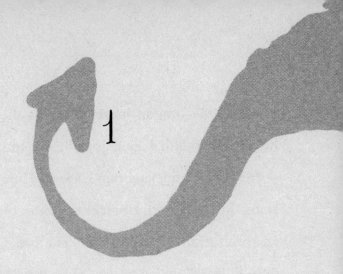

1

DAREK POINTED A STICK TOWARD
the sky. He swung it in two wide circles, then slowly
lowered it until its point touched the ground.
Above his head, Zantor soared, following the pat-
tern Darek had traced in the air. The dragonling
circled once, then twice over the paddock. Then
he swooped down for a landing.

"Hooray!" Darek shouted. He and his best
friend, Pola, clapped excitedly. "That was perfect!"

The little dragon barreled across the field in his funny, lopsided gait. Joyfully, he hurled himself at Darek, knocking him backward into the dirt. Darek squirmed with laughter as Zantor covered his face with kisses, *Thwip! Thwip!* The forked tongue tickled! Darek pulled a sugar cube from his pocket and tossed it a few feet away. The dragon scuffled after it, and Darek got to his feet and dusted himself off. Pola was still laughing, but he wasn't the only one, Darek realized. He turned and saw that he, Pola, and Zantor had an audience. A group of village children were hanging over the paddock fence.

"Zantor! Zantor, come here!" they cried, reaching out eager hands. When Zantor waddled over to play, the children shrieked with delight. "Let me pet him first!" one cried out. "No, me! No, me!" the others shouted.

Darek frowned. He was pleased, of course, that the villagers had finally accepted Zantor. For a time, it had seemed that they wouldn't even let him *live*. But Zantor had proven to all that he was both peaceful and courageous, and now they were willing to let him live among them. In fact, Zantor had become so popular lately that Darek seemed to be forever fighting for the dragonling's attention. Darek was the one who had found Zantor, after all, and brought him to the village. Why should he have to share him now with people who hadn't even wanted him at first? It didn't seem fair.

"Hey." Pola nudged Darek in the ribs. "Look who's here."

Darek looked where Pola had nodded. A taller girl had joined the other children. Her long, dark hair fell over her shoulders as she reached out and scratched the horn nubs on Zantor's head.

Zantor buried his face in the girl's shining hair and *thrummed* happily. Darek's frown deepened. "Rowena," he said with a groan.

Pola grinned. "I think she likes you," he said. "She's always hanging around lately."

"It's not me she likes, it's *him,*" Darek said. "Besides, who cares?"

"She's awful pretty," Pola teased.

"Yeah," Darek agreed, "and she's awful headstrong, stuck-up, and spoiled."

Pola laughed. "Maybe you'd be headstrong, stuck-up, and spoiled, too, if *your* father was Chief Elder."

Darek snorted. Then, as he watched Zantor playing with Rowena, a strange thing began to happen. Happy little thoughts started pushing into

Darek's head. They seemed to swell and pop, one after another, like bubbles. For a moment, Darek swore he could smell the perfume of Rowena's hair. He could almost feel the touch of her hands. Then, just as quickly as the funny feelings had come, they were gone. Confused, Darek shook his head.

"What's wrong?" Pola asked.

"I . . . it's weird," Darek said. "I felt like I was inside Zantor's head for a minute."

Pola looked over at Zantor and Rowena and laughed out loud. "Sounds like wishful thinking to me," he said. Then he gave Darek another poke.

Darek's frown returned. If he *had* been inside Zantor's head, he didn't like what he had felt there. Zantor was growing way too fond of Rowena. "Zantor!" he shouted. "Get back over here."

Rowena wound her arms tightly around the dragon. Zantor glanced over at Darek but didn't try to break free.

"Now!" Darek boomed.

With a sudden jerk, Zantor broke away from Rowena. He scuffled over to Darek as fast as his little legs would carry him. Darek looked at Rowena and grinned, as if to say, "See, he's all mine." Rowena glared back, tossing her head.

"I was just petting him," she called. "You don't have to be so mean about it."

"Zantor's not a pet," Darek snapped. "He and I have work to do. If you want to pet something, go pet a yuke."

Rowena glared a moment longer, then turned and stormed away.

Pola looked at Darek and shook his head.

"What's wrong with you?" Darek asked.

"You have a funny way of showing a girl that you like her," Pola said.

"I *don't* like her," Darek insisted. "She's nothing but a pest."

"Oh, yeah?" Pola said. He laughed and pointed to Zantor. The dragonling was still gazing, dreamy-eyed, after Rowena. "Doesn't look like Zantor agrees with you."

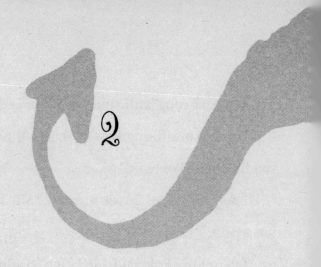

2

"YOU SHOULD HAVE SEEN ZANTOR today," Darek said to his mother and father and his brother, Clep, over dinner. "He's learning so fast! He takes off and lands on command. He can fly a circle and a figure eight . . ."

Hearing his name, Zantor uncurled himself from the hearth. He shuffled over and nuzzled Darek's arm. *"Thrumm,"* he sang happily at Darek's elbow. Darek smiled and slipped him a spoonful of barliberry pudding.

Darek's mother, Alayah, attempted to frown.

"No feeding the dragon at the table," she reminded her son.

Darek's father ate quietly. He listened but did not respond to Darek's chatter. Yanek had come to accept Zantor. He even loved the little dragon, but at the same time he had doubts about Darek's dream. A future where people and dragons lived peacefully, side by side, helping each other?

"It's a nice idea," Yanek would say when Darek pressed him about it. "But such things are not always as simple as they seem."

It was true that such things *weren't* simple. Darek had learned that the hard way. When his father had allowed Darek to bring Zantor back to Zoriak, the villagers had been very angry. They had almost burned Yanek at the stake! But Darek and Zantor had proved to the villagers that they were wrong about dragons. One day, Darek was sure, he and Zantor would prove his father wrong about the future, too.

Darek turned toward his big brother. "Hurry and finish eating, Clep," he said. "I want to show you everything Zantor learned today."

Clep was just swallowing his last spoonful of pudding when a sharp rap came on the door.

"I'll get it," Darek said, jumping up.

He pulled the door open, then stepped back in surprise. "Excellency," he said, bowing low. The Chief Elder himself stood on their doorstep.

Darek's parents and Clep quickly rose to their feet.

His mother rushed forward. "Enter, Sire," she

said. "Please take some supper with us."

"I have already supped, Alayah," the Elder said. He nodded stiffly to them all. "I have come to have a word with Yanek."

"Of course." Darek's father bowed and led the way to the front parlor.

Darek and Clep glanced uneasily at each other.

Alayah twisted her apron in her hands. "I hope this visit does not bode ill," she whispered to her sons.

"As you know," they overheard the Chief Elder say, "my daughter's Decanum approaches."

Darek sighed a sigh of relief. So that was all. The Chief Elder had come to talk over the arrangements for Rowena's Decanum. The whole village was soon to celebrate her tenth birthday. There would be a full parade, a banquet, and a formal ball. Darek's father, as Chief Marksman and Captain of the

Guard, would have much to do to prepare.

Darek's mother seemed relieved, too. She went back to the table to finish her pudding.

"You know, Darek," she said with a teasing smile, "there has been much talk in the village. Everyone is wondering who Rowena will choose to be her escort for the Decanum Ball."

Darek's face reddened. Rowena's escort? What was his mother getting at?

"Have *you* any idea who her escort will be?" she asked.

"Not at all," Darek answered shortly.

Clep grinned. "I've heard some names mentioned, Mother," he said. "One very familiar name, in fact." He shot a teasing glance at Darek. "Perhaps that explains the Chief Elder's visit, eh?"

Darek gave Clep such a look of dismay that

Clep had to laugh out loud. "It's not the end of the world, little brother," he said. "I can think of fates worse than having to dance with the lovely Rowena."

"Why don't *you* escort her if you think she's so lovely?" Darek snapped. "I think she's a spoiled brat."

"Hush, you two!" Alayah whispered. "Have you forgotten who speaks with your father in the next room?"

Zantor bounced over and butted Darek in the arm. Glad of the interruption, Darek went to the cupboard. He took out the dragonling's bowl and began to prepare his supper.

"It makes no difference what you think, Darek," Clep said in a more serious voice. "You will, of course, accept if you are asked."

Darek didn't answer. He filled Zantor's bowl

with fallow meal and barliberries. Then he ladled warm water over all and stirred it into a mash. The smell of it suddenly made his stomach growl hungrily. He raised the bowl to his lips and took a big gulp.

"Blaah!" It tasted awful. Darek spit the mash back into the bowl and stared at it. What on Zoriak had possessed him to eat Zantor's food? He'd just finished eating his own dinner! And even if he was hungry, he would never eat fallow meal mash! He looked up and saw Clep and his mother staring at him strangely.

"What *are* you doing?" his mother asked.

Zantor butted Darek's arm again, nearly upsetting the bowl. Darek lowered it slowly to the floor. The dragonling dived eagerly for the food, gulping and gulping. Slowly, the hunger pangs in Darek's stomach began to subside.

"I know what he's doing, Mother," Clep said. "He's trying to change the subject."

"What subject?" Darek mumbled, still staring at Zantor. The dish was nearly empty now, and Darek was feeling quite full. A bubble swelled and swelled in his stomach. It wiggled its way up through his chest and burst from his mouth. "Buurp!"

"Darek!" his mother exclaimed.

Darek clapped a hand over his mouth. "Sorry," he muttered. What was happening to him?

Clep frowned and shook his head. "Why would anyone want to go to the ball with a dragon-wit like you, anyway?" he asked.

"I'm sure Rowena *doesn't* want to go with me,"

Darek retorted. "Why do you even listen to those stupid rumors?"

"*Ahem.*"

Darek looked up at the sound of the deep voice. His father's broad frame filled the doorway. He was staring at Darek with a serious look on his face.

"You had better come in here, son," he said. "The Chief Elder's mission today concerns you."